The Best
Colors

WRITTEN AND ILLUSTRATED BY

BARBARA TAFF

This book is dedicated to Ann Jackowitz for her unrelenting support and belief in me.

Once upon a time, there was a color named Red that was full of itself.

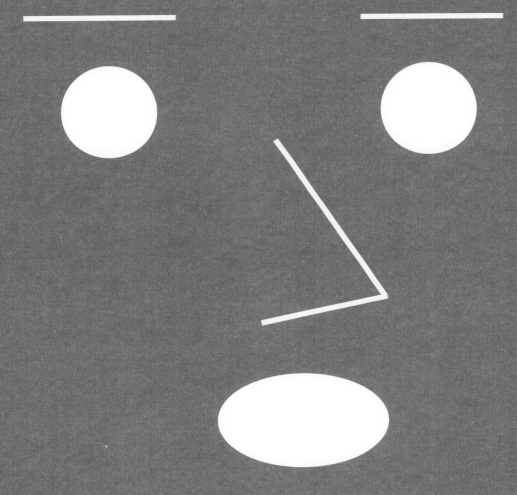

"I'm the best color in the whole world," said Red.

Along came Yellow who had a different opinion.

"I'm Yellow – the brightest color in the rainbow. If any color is the best, it's me!"

"No, I'm the best because I'm passionate, exciting and daring," said Red.

"**Clearly, I'm too enlightened to argue with you. You see, I'm Yellow, the color of the sun,**

the moon and the stars."

"Everyone takes those things for granted. But, I'm Red and nobody takes me for granted. I'm the strongest, most energetic color and I get **NOTICED!**"

"I'm the color of stop signs,

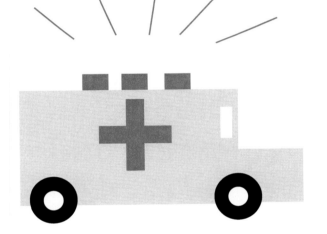

an ambulance's flashing lights,

and fire-engines," said Red.

"I'll have you know that I'm the color of lemonade and yellow gold," bragged Yellow.

"And, I'm the yellow in the Yellow Rose of Texas. **YEEHAW!!"**

"I'm the color of radishes and red peppers and ketchup!" shouted Red.

"I'm the color of corn and yellow peppers and mustard!" hollered Yellow.

Then, from out of the blue, another color appeared.

"Hold it, hold it! You're both wrong!!!

I'm the best!"

said the new color.

"Oh, no, you're not!" said Red.

"Who are you?" asked Yellow.

"Why, I'm Royal Blue, the most aristocratic color. I'm blue-blooded you know," said Blue proudly.

"I love your red cape," said Red. "That's a terrific yellow crown," added Yellow. "But what makes you think you're the best?" asked the two colors in unison.

and the water in all the lakes, rivers and oceans," said Blue, quietly standing on a cloud.

"I'm Blue,
the color of the
Blue Ribbon!"

"Big Deal!"
Red screamed
with jealousy.

"Look Red, don't take losing so hard." said Blue calmly.

"I'll show you who the real winner is!" said Red.

"Hold it!" interrupted Yellow who stood nose to nose with Red. **"This isn't worth fighting over. Can't we all just get along?"**

"Fine by me." agreed Blue.

When Yellow and Red stepped back from each other, they were surprised to see that something was left on the tip of their noses!

"I'll go see if I can find out what that is," said Blue.

"I found out on the Internet that red and yellow make the color orange," said Blue.

Yellow and Red had created a new color and hugged joyfully!

And, the most INCREDIBLE thing happened!

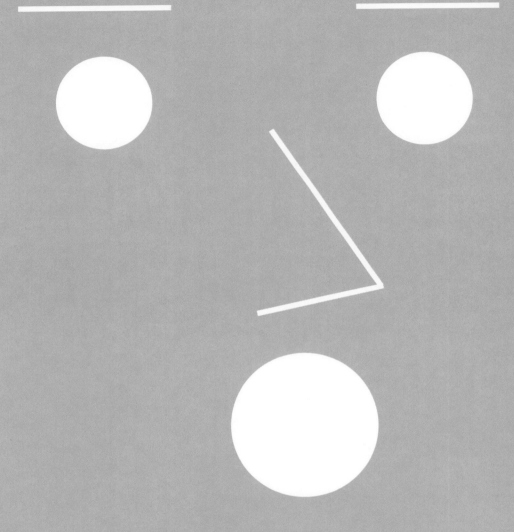

The two colors became one color!
Yellow and Red completely disappeared
into ORANGE!

Blue turned pale in shock!

"What did you do with Red and Yellow?" Blue asked Orange.

"I don't know what you're talking about, dude. I'm, like, my own color. Red and Yellow might have started me, but, they're, like, gone," said Orange.

Feeling sad, Blue started to walk home and, as Blue turned the corner…

Blue saw Red and Yellow sharing an Orange drink together.

Blue was happy to see friends again.

"Where did
you and Red go?"
Blue asked Yellow.

"We went shopping for red and yellow paint so that we could re-color ourselves," explained Yellow.

"Hey," said Blue. "Do you think we could make a new color?"

"Sure," answered Yellow and gave Blue a big hug. And, the most REMARKABLE thing happened...

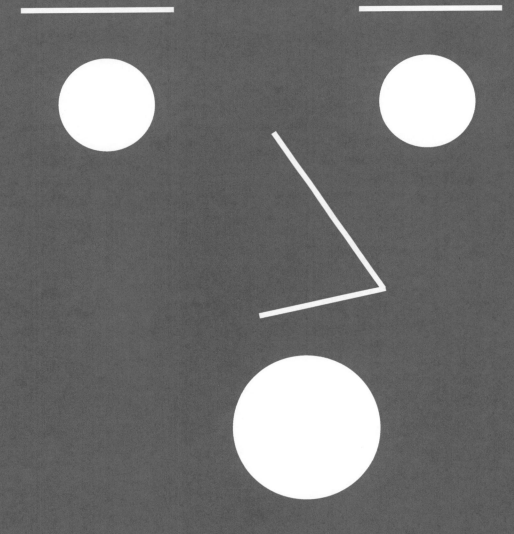

The two colors became one color! Yellow and Blue completely disappeared into GREEN!

Later, Red and Blue hugged. And, the most AMAZING thing happened...

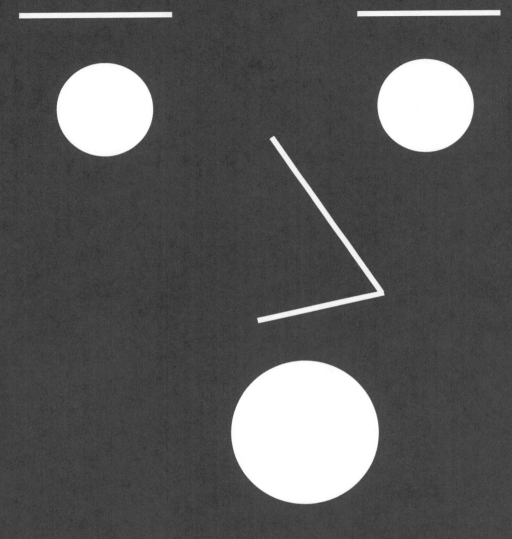

**The two colors became one color!
Red and Blue completely disappeared
into PURPLE!**

The next day, Blue, Red and Yellow went to visit their new creations, Purple, Orange and Green.

Red, Yellow and Blue found Orange, Green and Purple bickering.

"Why certainly, I'm the best because I'm funny, zany and the color of **PASSION FRUIT!**" said Purple.

I love you!

I love you more!

"No way. I'm Orange, the best color because there would be no pumpkins, carrots or FIRE without me!"

"Hold it! You're both wrong, I'm the best. I'm the color of rolling hills and the green grass on golf courses and the leaves on trees." said Green.

"I think it's time we all tell them who's the **best color,**" said Blue.

The End

Suggested Activities

Materials: Water-based paints, crayons, paper and brushes

Mix Colors

Use the colors Red, Yellow and Blue to make Orange, Green and Purple
by mixing the color combinations shown in the story.

Express Emotions with Color

What colors are you when feeling angry, happy, sad, and quiet?

The Color Around Us

1. Paint pictures of all the green foods you can think of.
2. What would you look like in an all purple silly outfit?

Have a Conversation on Diversity

In the book, all the colors want to be best color.
Is there such a thing as a best color?

Barbara Taff

A mixed-media artist, Taff unites her expertise in cartooning, graphic design, writing and teaching in *The Best Colors*. An award-winning graphic designer and creator of whimsical scenario sculptures, she has exhibited her work nationally. She holds a master's degree in art education from Pratt Institute in New York, and her articles on art activities for children have appeared in national art education publications. Born in Rochester, N.Y., Taff lives in New York City and Fleischmanns, N.Y. She can be contacted at bt@btaffdesign.com.

Made in the USA
Lexington, KY
01 September 2018